Published by
Princeton Architectural Press
202 Warren Street
Hudson, New York 12534
www.papress.com

First published in French under the title:
Les ombres de Nasla
Cécile Roumiguière, Simone Rea
© Éditions du Seuil, 2019, 57 rue Gaston Tessier, 75019 Paris

English Edition © 2020 Princeton Architectural Press
All rights reserved.
Printed and bound in Portugal
23 22 21 20 4 3 2 1 First edition

ISBN 978-1-61689-950-9

This book was illustrated using oil paints.

Editor: Kristen Hewitt
Typesetting: Natalie Snodgrass

Library of Congress Cataloging-in-Publication Data available upon request.

CÉCILE ROUMIGUIÈRE
ISTRATIONS BY SIMONE REA

NASLA'S DREAM

PRINCETON ARCHITECTURAL PRESS
NEW YORK

Nasla is not asleep.

Lying in her bed, she sees a yellow dot above the wardrobe.

A little eye, like an opening in the dark night.

Nasla wonders who is looking at her.

Is it her toy turtle?

Yesterday, Nasla decided she was too old to sleep with
stuffed animals, so she asked her father to put it away
on top of the wardrobe.

Her turtle is probably not very happy, but a stuffed animal,
even an angry one, does not usually stare like that.

Nasla wants to sing,
but at night, you do not sing.
At night, you sleep.

But what if the yellow dot
grows and grows? What if
it becomes big enough to
swallow her whole?

She would not be able
to sleep or sing.

Nasla stares at the wardrobe and sees a shadow.

When her father put her turtle up there, he also
placed Timboubou the elephant, and all of Nasla's toys—
the mushroom castle, the hippo with a broken foot,
the giant ant, the toy garage, the broken dolls,
and the red truck—in a nice neat pile.

The shadow moves.

Timboubou is swinging his trunk!

Nasla wants to tell Timboubou and her turtle
and all her toys that she is a big girl now.

She wants to tell them that they will be happy,
all together on top of the wardrobe.

Nasla wants to talk to her toys, but at night,
you don't talk. At night, you sleep.

At night, only the Moon is allowed to shine—
yellow, red, or silver.

At night, the Moon can do whatever it wants.

Nasla wants to play with the Moon.

But at night, you do not play. At night, you sleep.

The yellow eye does not sleep.

It watches Nasla.

Timboubou does not sleep either.
He swings his trunk from side to side.

What if the shadow is not her toy elephant, but
a ghost with long arms? A giant squid with tentacles?

Now Nasla hears a sound,
something breathing in the dark.

It is not her turtle. It is not Timboubou.
But what, then?

Nasla slips her hand under her pillow.
There, she keeps her secret charm for warding
off yellow eyes, elephant trunks, tentacles,
and strange sounds in the night–

a small blanket her mother gave her when
she was a baby.

Nasla's blanket makes the yellow eye less bright and makes the shadows disappear.

And that's when Nasla falls asleep.
In a dream, she is surrounded by all of her old toys.
They dance around a bonfire, climb trees, and make
a big messy pile.

On the wardrobe, the cat stretches. She's tired of playing with the trunk of the toy elephant. Softly, she jumps to the floor, is illuminated by the Moon, blinks her yellow eye at the turtle, and goes out.